this

little ORCHARD

book belongs to

· ·

· ·

ORCHARD BOOKS
96 Leonard Street, London EC2A 4RH
Hachette Children's Books
Level 17/207 Kent Street, Sydney NSW 2000
1 84362 224 6
First published in Great Britain in 1998
This edition published in 2003
Illustrations © Penny Dann 1998
The right of Penny Dann to be identified as
the illustrator of this work has been asserted by her
in accordance with the Copyright, Designs and Patents Act, 1988.
A CIP catalogue record for this book is available from the British Library.
3 5 7 9 10 8 6 4
Printed in China

The wheels on the bus

Penny Dann

little 🌳 ORCHARD

The wheels on the bus go round and round
Round and round
Round and round

The wheels on the bus go
Round and round
All day long.

The people on the bus step **on and off**
On and off
On and off

The people on the bus step
On and off
All day long.

The driver on the bus says Move along, please!
Move along, please!
Move along, please!

The driver on the bus says
Move along, please!
All day long.

The riders on the bus go **bumpety-bump**
Bumpety-bump
Bumpety-bump

The riders on the bus go **bumpety-bump**
All day long.

bumpety-bump bumpety-bump

The children on the bus go **chatter chatter chatter**
Chatter chatter chatter
Chatter chatter chatter

The children on the bus go **chatter chatter chatter**
All day long.

The babies on the bus go
Wah! Wah! Wah!
Wah! Wah! Wah!
Wah! Wah! Wah!

The babies on the bus go
Wah! Wah! Wah!
All day long.

The parents on the bus go Sshh! Sshh! Sshh!
Sshh! Sshh! Sshh!
Sshh! Sshh! Sshh!

The parents on the bus go
Sshh! Sshh! Sshh!
All day long.

The wipers on the bus go
Swish swish swish
Swish swish swish
Swish swish swish

The wipers on the bus go
Swish swish swish
All day long.